Folk Tales of
SOUTH
AMERICA

Retold by Sheila Hatherley

Illustrated by Pat Reynolds

Evans

Titles in this Evans Folk Tales series are:

China   North America

Japan   South America

First published in the U.K. in 1993 by
Evans Brothers Limited,
2a Portman Mansions,
Chiltern Street,
London WIM ILE.

ISBN 0 237 51309 9

First published in Australia in 1991 by
The Macmillan Company of Australia Pty Ltd
107 Moray Street, South Melbourne 3205
6 Clarke Street, Crows Nest 2065

Set in Bookman by
Superskill Graphics, Singapore
Printed in Hong Kong

Contents

Lucia and the Great Snake

A Story from Chile

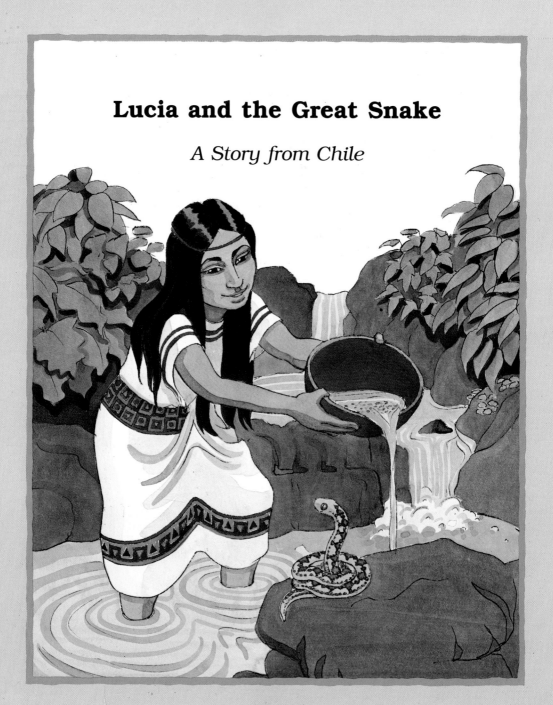

Long ago a widow and her only daughter lived in a little village on the coast of Chile. They were very poor and often had nothing to eat. One day the woman managed to find some grain which she hoped to cook for their supper.

'It's not very good grain,' she sighed. 'It looks like the sweepings from the granary floor and it is full of sand.'

'Never mind, Mother. I will wash it in the stream,' her daughter, Lucia, offered, 'then it will be fit to cook.'

As she rinsed the sandy grain in the clear water she saw a little, yellow snake curled up on a stone, watching her.

'You pretty little creature!' she said. 'I'll take you home with me and you shall be my pet.'

Back at her house she hunted around until she found an old clay pot to make a home for her new pet. After she and her mother had eaten their supper she scraped the pan and gave the few bits left to the snake.

Each day after that she found some crumbs of food, no matter how small, to share with the yellow snake. Her new pet seemed quite happy to stay with her and grew fat on the scraps she gave it. Soon it grew too large for the clay pot and Lucia found an old barrel to replace it, but soon the snake had outgrown that, too. At last the snake said that it would be best if it went away and found its own home.

'I've grown so large I just don't fit into my barrel any more. In any case, it must be very difficult for you to find enough food for me. I must go away.'

Lucia was very upset, because she had grown so fond of her pet.

'Don't cry!' the snake told her. 'You have been very good to me. Now I have a magic gift for you, so that you will never be poor again. Rub my eyes with your fingers, then whenever you wash your hands and shake them, gold coins will drop from your finger tips.'

Lucia gently rubbed her fingers over the snake's eyes before she said goodbye to it. After the snake had gone she washed her hands and shook them. Gold coins dropped from the ends of her fingers, just as the snake had promised.

'Mother! Mother, come quickly and see what has happened,' she cried. 'We need never be poor or hungry again.'

They tried to keep their good fortune a secret, but that was not easy to do in a small village. Soon the news spread through the countryside that the widow had a beautiful daughter with magic powers. Even the King heard about her.

'If I can find this young woman I will marry her,' he decided.

He asked a witch to help him find this wonderful girl.

'I will pay you well if you succeed,' he promised her.

Very soon the witch discovered where Lucia lived and went to the girl's mother.

'The King has heard about your daughter's magic powers and wants to speak to her.'

Lucia's mother was worried by this news, but the witch promised to accompany Lucia to see the King and then bring her safely back again.

'She will be quite safe with me. I'll guard her as if she was my own child!'

The witch, however, had secret plans. She had a daughter, too, a girl about the same age as Lucia. On the journey to see the King the witch grabbed Lucia and threw magic dust in her eyes to make her blind. Then she pushed her over a cliff into the sea to drown.

'Now,' she cried, 'I will tell the King that my daughter is the girl with the magic powers and she, not Lucia, will marry the King!'

But Lucia did not drown. As she was swept out to sea some fishermen saw her and rescued her. They took her back to the hut where they lived, and bathed and bandaged her blind eyes. They gave her food and found her a place to sleep, and she stayed with the fishermen for some time.

Then one day she heard a voice calling, 'Lucia, what has happened to you? Why are you living here?'

It was her pet snake, now grown to an enormous size.

'Oh, how good it is to meet you again,' she sobbed as she stroked the creature's great sides. Then she told it all that had happened to her. 'I cannot find my way home,' she said 'because I am blind. Please help me!'

The snake answered, 'You took great care of me when I was small. Now it will give me great pleasure to help you. Close your eyes, then reach out and touch my eyes.'

Lucia did as she was told.

'I can see! I can see!' she cried in delight. 'Oh, thank you, dear snake!'

'Now jump on my back and I will take you home,' it said.

Lucia said goodbye to the fishermen who had cared for her, climbed onto the snake's broad back and in next to no time was back at home with her mother. The widow was overjoyed to see her daughter again, for she had believed she was dead. Soon all the village heard her story and joined in welcoming her home.

By this time the witch's daughter had married the King, but all was not going well for her. No matter how often she washed her hands, not a single gold coin fell from her fingers.

'I must have lost my magic power when I married you, sire,' she told the King as an excuse.

When the King finally heard of Lucia's return home he realised that he had been tricked, and he was furiously angry. The following week he gave a great feast and invited all the people from the nearby villages. Everyone came and enjoyed a wonderful meal with all kinds of roasted meat dishes followed by rich desserts, dripping with cream and honey.

The King watched all his guests very carefully. Little fingerbowls of water were placed on the tables, so that the guests could rinse their sticky fingers. When Lucia dipped her fingertips into the water and shook her hands, the droplets turned to gold coins.

The King rushed to Lucia's side and asked her the meaning of this strange happening. She told him about the snake, it's magic gift to her and how she had suffered at the hands of the witch. She told him, too, of the kind fishermen who had saved her.

'The witch and her daughter shall be punished!' the King cried. 'They have caused you great suffering and they have tricked and cheated me, their King. They deserve to be thrown into the deepest dungeon! Seize them!'

But it was too late. They had already vanished and were never seen again.

In time Lucia married the King and they had a happy life together. But Lucia never forgot her good friend, the snake, and the fishermen who had helped her.

Pariacaca

A Story from Peru

Long ago, when the world was still being made, five mysterious eggs appeared on the top of Mount Condorcoto. Five falcons hatched from the eggs, and in time the five birds turned into men. They were sun-gods, and they went through the world doing marvellous deeds. The eldest of the five brothers was called Pariacaca. He ruled over the winds of heaven and the rains and floods.

Pariacaca often wandered through the world to see how men and women were using the land they had been given, and if they were treating one another with kindness and generosity. On these occasions he always disguised himself, so that he could see people as they really were, and not behaving in some special way to impress him, a sun-god.

Sometimes he dressed in rags and became an old beggar. As he went from town to town, and even from village to village, he was disappointed to see how selfish and greedy people were. Many seemed to think only of themselves, and did not spare so much as a kind word for those who were less fortunate than they were. Ragged, old men, such as he often appeared to be, were often pushed out of the way, and spoken to roughly and scornfully.

One day he sat down to rest in the marketplace of a small town. It was a prosperous little town nestling at the foot of the mountains. The land round the town was watered by a stream which was fed by a large lake up in the mountains. Summer and winter the water tumbled down the mountain side from a crack in the rock walls of the lake. This meant that the farmers could grow a variety of crops, which they brought to the town to sell.

Pariacaca saw that it had been market day, and the people who had sold their produce were sitting around talking and drinking chicha, their favourite drink. Nobody offered him anything to eat or drink, or took even the slightest notice of him. He sat under a tree, tired, dusty and friendless.

Then a young woman walked past and felt sorry for him, and ashamed of the selfish townspeople. She bought a bowl of chicha and gave it to him.

'Old man, you look hot and tired. Drink this, it will refresh you.'

'Thank you, young woman. You are much kinder than the rest of the people in this town.'

Pariacaca drank the chicha, and while he did so he looked up at the mountain range above the town and the tumbling stream.

'Listen carefully to what I say,' he told the girl, 'and do exactly what I tell you. This town is going to be destroyed. There is so much water in the lake up there, that the rocks will not be able to hold it back. You and your family must leave here immediately and go up over the mountains to safety. I tell you this because of your generosity towards a poor, old man.'

The girl believed his warning, and persuaded her parents and brother to leave the town that night. When they reached the lake above the town they were horrified to see the rocks give way and water and mud rush down the mountain side. The town they had just left was buried under a huge pile of mud and stones.

The girl and her family continued on over the mountain. The people who lived on the other side of the range were full of sympathy when they heard about the landslide burying their town. They gave them a place to live and allowed them to work in their fields. But soon they had no water, because the lake which had burst its banks had supplied water to both sides of the mountain. The crops of maize began to wither and die.

One morning, as the girl sat crying beside the ruined crops, Pariacaca, still disguised as an old beggar, came and spoke to her.

'What is the matter?' he asked her. 'Why are you crying?'

'Because we have no water for our crops,' she told him.

'When I was thirsty you gave me a bowl of chicha,' Pariacaca said. 'Now I will give you water to save your crops, but only on condition that you promise to marry me.'

'The people here have been good to my family. They cared for us when we were homeless. If you can promise that there will always be water for their fields, I will gladly marry you,' she told him.

'You really would marry an old, ragged beggarman?' Pariacaca asked in surprise.

'I am quite willing to be the wife of a wandering beggar, even if you are old enough to be my grandfather,' she promised him.

Pariacaca went up into the mountains to where the lake had been. It was now just a gaping, muddy hole. He called to the birds and animals who were his friends and set them to work. Some of them were to collect pebbles, clods of earth and even grains of sand, and build a great dam where the landslide had taken place. Others were to dig a channel  at the other end of the lake, running down to where the people's crops were dying. All this was done in only a few minutes. Then Pariacaca used his great powers to flood the lake with water once more. Because of the dam

which the birds and animals had built, the town buried under the mud received no water. The new channel sent water bubbling down to the parched fields where the young girl and her family waited.

When Pariacaca came back down the mountain the young girl ran to him joyfully.

'Thank you, thank you! Dear old man! You have saved the crops of these good people who helped my family, and now I am ready to keep my promise and marry you.'

Pariacaca smiled and straightened up his bent body. He threw off his disguise and appeared as his true self. He was once again the young, handsome sun-god.

'You were willing to marry a wandering beggar, but your sweet and generous heart makes me ask if you will be the bride of Pariacaca, the sun-god?'

True to his promise, that valley has never since lacked water, and is one of the most fertile parts of Peru.

The Great Flood

A Story from Ecuador

Near Quito, in Ecuador, there is a district called Canaribamba and the Indians who live there are called Canaris. The Canaris believe that their race has descended from a beautiful macaw parrot, and this is how it happened.

Many hundreds of years ago there was an immense flood which covered the whole land. It rained and rained without ceasing for days, and then weeks. Crops were ruined, animals and people drowned and whole villages were swept away in the raging waters.

Two brothers who lived near the coast were fortunate enough to own a small boat.

'We must try to reach higher ground,' Elder Brother said, as they watched the torrents tearing away at the land. 'If we don't, then we too will die.'

So they packed the boat with food and other necessities and set out towards a mountain peak called Huacaynan. They paddled for days, and often their little boat was in danger of capsizing in the swirling waters. After many adventures they reached the mountain, but already the water was more than halfway up its steep sides.

Thankfully, they dragged the boat up onto the mountain side.

'If we turn it upside down, the boat will give us some sort of shelter,' Younger Brother suggested.

'But for how long?' Elder Brother asked miserably. 'The water is still rising, and we are almost on the mountain peak.'

By morning the flood was lapping at their feet.

'We are going to drown,' moaned Elder Brother, 'there is nowhere else to go.'

'Look!' his brother cried in amazement. 'The mountain has grown! It is much higher than it was last evening, so let us move further up to the new ground.'

Each night after that the mountain grew, so that there was always enough land left for them to live in safety, even though the flood was still rising.

By the time the deluge had ended all their supply of food had been eaten. As the water gradually went down they built a little hut from branches of trees they dragged from the water. It was a rough little shelter, but it was better than the upturned boat. Since they had no other food they tried to find enough roots and seeds to keep them alive. It was a miserable existence, scratching through the mud trying to find enough to eat. Each day saw them becoming weaker and thinner, until they feared they would die of starvation.

Then one day they returned to their hut empty-handed and hungry, for they had found nothing at all to eat. To their amazement there was a wonderful meal cooked and waiting for them. There was even chicha to drink. Chicha is something like beer, and is made from fermented maize.

'Where has all this come from?' Younger Brother cried. 'There is nobody living on this mountain but us!'

'Let us eat! We can discover later who has been so good to us,' his brother replied, cramming his mouth full of delicious food.

But after nearly two weeks they were no nearer to solving the mystery. Each night when they returned to the hut they found a meal cooked and ready to be eaten. Who was helping them, they wondered? Where were they finding such marvellous food in the ruined countryside?

'There is one way to discover who is being so good to us. They always come when the hut is empty and we are both out looking for food. Today I will stay behind and keep watch, while you, Younger Brother, go in search of food alone,' Elder Brother decided.

He hid himself behind the hut and waited. Soon he was surprised to see two huge parrots, called macaws, alight nearby. They were dressed like Canaris and were carrying baskets of food. They went into the hut and started to prepare the food for cooking. The young man's surprise was even greater when the largest macaw took off her cloak. He saw she had the face of a beautiful young woman.

He jumped from his hiding place, wanting to thank the strange beings for their kindness. His sudden appearance in the doorway startled the macaws, and without waiting for him to speak they flew away with loud cries. The baskets of food vanished, too.

When Younger Brother returned to the hut that evening he was disappointed and angry.

'What, no food? Not even a drop of chicha to quench my thirst after a long, wretched day? What happened?'

His brother told him about the strange, beautiful parrots and how they flew away when he approached them.

'You must have frightened them very badly. In future I will keep watch, and you can look for food. I do hope they come back, because if they don't I fear we are going to be very hungry.'

For three days Younger Brother hid behind the door of the hut and waited. Nothing happened. Then the next day his patience was rewarded. The two macaws returned with baskets of food.

Younger Brother watched quietly while they prepared the food. Then, when it was cooked, he sprang out and slammed the door shut, imprisoning the birds. They were very angry and fought wildly to get free. The larger macaw managed to break free from his grasp and flew away, however he clung tightly to the smaller macaw and held it captive.

Gradually he was able to calm the bird and it stopped trying to escape. He told it quietly that he did not wish to harm it, but he and his brother only wanted to thank the macaws for helping them when they were starving. It was then that he saw the macaw was really a young woman.

'You are very beautiful,' he told her at last.

'And you are very handsome,' she replied.

Of course, Younger Brother and the macaw-girl fell deeply in love. When Elder Brother returned to the hut he was sad to hear that the largest macaw had flown away. It would have been wonderful if that bird, too, had turned into a beautiful young woman, and had stayed with him. Unhappily, it was never seen again.

Younger Brother made the macaw-girl his wife and they lived together on the mountain for many years. Elder Brother stayed with them, and they all worked together to build a new life from the ruins left behind by the great flood.

Each day the macaw flew out and hunted over the countryside for grain and seeds, which together they sowed to grow crops and fruit. Soon they had plenty to eat, so there was no need for any more magical feasts.

As years passed Younger Brother and the macaw-girl had a large family, six sons and six daughters, and it is from them that all the Canaris are descended. They still look on the mountain as a very special place, or huaca. They pay special respect to all macaws and their bright feathers are greatly prized and used in their festivals.

Coniraya and Cavillaca

A Story from Peru

In ancient times in Peru, long before the famous Inca nation became known, great beings came to earth from the sun. These sun-gods were very powerful. They created many things that the mortals lacked and taught them new skills to make their lives easier.

One of these sun-gods was named Coniraya. It was he who first taught people to build terraces on the hillsides so that they could grow more crops. He showed them, too, how to dig channels to carry water to their plants. Few people realised that Coniraya was a sun-god because he kept his identity secret. He lived on earth as a poor man dressed in rags and was despised by most people, even by other sun-gods.

Coniraya fell in love with a beautiful woman called Cavillaca, who was also from the sun, but she thought such a poor, ragged man was beneath her notice. Using his great powers, Coniraya gave her a magical fruit from a lumca tree. This strange fruit caused her to become pregnant, and she bore a son.

Cavillaca realised that she had been tricked into having a child, and that only another sun-god could have done such a thing. She called a great meeting of all the sun-gods she knew to celebrate her son's first birthday, for she knew that the child, being born of a sun-god, would recognise his own father. She put the baby on the ground and at once he crawled over to Coniraya, who was sitting apart from all the others at the celebration. Cavillaca was angry and ashamed that the baby had claimed such a poor, ragged creature as his father, and the next day she vanished from home, taking the child with her.

'If only she had waited until I had told her who I really was!' Coniraya cried. 'If only she could have accepted me as a poor man! Now I must find her and bring her and the child back at all costs. That child is my son.'

As he travelled in search of Cavillaca he asked the animals and birds he met along the way to help him.

'She and the child are not far away. They are travelling towards the coast and you should soon catch up with them,' the condor told him.

'Thank you, great bird,' Coniraya said. 'Because you have been willing to help me in my search I will give your wings great strength. From now on you shall soar over mountains and ravines and build your nest in high places where nothing can harm it.'

Coniraya went on his way full of hope.

Next he met a fox sunning itself on the river bank.

'Have you seen Cavillaca and her child pass this way?' he asked.

'What if I have? What do you want with them?' the fox jeered. 'A ragged beggar like you!'

'Because of your ill will you shall be disliked and hunted by all people. I curse you, fox!' he told the animal.

As he went on his way he saw a falcon hunting for food.

'Bird, have you seen anyone pass this way? I am looking for a young woman and a little child,' Coniraya said. 'The condor told me they were travelling towards the sea.'

'No, I haven't seen them,' the bird told him. 'But I've been hunting for food for my chicks, so they could easily have passed this way without me seeing them. I'll fly on ahead, and if I see them I'll come back and tell you.'

'Thank you, falcon. Because you are so helpful from now on I will give you keen eyesight and your flight shall be as swift as the wind.'

So Coniraya hurried on and the falcon flew ahead, but it could see no trace of Cavillaca.

Next Coniraya saw a flock of parrots feeding in a tree and asked them if they had seen Cavillaca. Their beaks were so full of seeds and fruit that they couldn't even answer him.

'Have you nothing to say?' Coniraya demanded.

Still the parrots went on feeding.

'Right! From this day on your voices will be so loud that your enemies will always find you, even when you are feeding. You are cursed, parrots!'

It was now late afternoon and the shadows were lengthening. Soon it would be night, and so far there was no trace of Cavillaca. Coniraya felt sad, for he loved her very much. The journey so far had been difficult and the road rough. Coniraya began to feel tired and low-spirited. Then he saw a mountain lion stretched out on a rocky outcrop.

'Have you seen a beautiful young woman pass this way carrying a little child?' he asked the animal.

'Yes, I have,' the mountain lion told him. 'They are not far away either, but it is too dark for you to find them now. Why don't you bathe your face in the stream and rest here for the night? They will have found shelter and be resting, too. You will certainly see them tomorrow.'

Coniraya was so grateful for the mountain lion's kindness that he blessed it with special powers.

'You, mountain lion, shall be respected and feared by all people. I appoint you as the executioner of evildoers. Even after death you shall be honoured. When they take your skin they shall not cut off the head, but shall preserve it, even the teeth and eyes, as if you

were still alive. Your paws and tail shall remain
hanging from the skin. At all the great festivals
people shall wear your skin over their heads
and sing and dance, so that you are given
honour.'

Coniraya stayed the night with the mountain lion and at dawn he set out again to find Cavillaca. He kept walking towards the coast. By noon he stood on a headland looking down at the sea and he thought he could make out the forms of Cavillaca and her child on the beach below. He called out to them.

'Come back, Cavillaca! Come back, my son!'

But it was too late. The young woman and her child had turned to stone. They had become two rocks with the waves lapping at their feet.

Coniraya lost Cavillaca and his son, but for many years he stayed on earth working great marvels and fighting many enemies. The condor is still able to soar higher and further than any other bird, and its mountain-top nest is safe from all its enemies. The falcon is known for its keen eyesight and swift flight. The fox is often disliked and hunted, and parrots' noisy voices can be heard from far away, even when they are feeding. Coniraya's decree about the mountain lion came true, too. For hundreds of years after this the animal was feared and honoured. Its skin, left whole and lifelike, was worn by special dancers at the great festivals, just as the sun-god had said it should be.